TALENT

001148455

D0484870

SPIRIT OF THE WEST

	DATE DUE		5 / 98
JUN 15 '98			
JUN 25 '98			
OCT 20 '98			
	WITHDRAWN		
	Damaged, Obsolete, or Surplus		
	Jackson County Library Services		
GAYLORD			PRINTED IN U.S.A.

liquid damage notes
p. 109-118
4-11

This book is part of the
TREASURED HORSES COLLECTION™
that is distributed with replica horses
in toy and hobby stores by
The ERTL Company, Incorporated.

Read all of the books in the
TREASURED HORSES COLLECTION™.

SPIRIT
OF THE WEST

*The story of an Appaloosa mare, her precious foal,
and the girl whose pride endangers them all*

Written by **Jahnna N. Malcolm**
Illustrated by **Sandy Rabinowitz**
Cover Illustration by **Christa Keiffer**
Developed by Nancy Hall, Inc.

Scholastic Inc.

New York   Toronto   London   Auckland   Sydney

ISBN 0-590-06866-0

Copyright © 1996 by Nancy Hall, Inc.
All rights reserved. Published by Scholastic Inc.,
555 Broadway, New York, NY 10012, by arrangement with
Nancy Hall, Inc. and The ERTL Company.

12 11 10 9 8 7 6 5 4 3   7 8 9/9 0 1 2/0

Printed in the U.S.A.   40

First Scholastic printing, January 1997

CONTENTS

CHAPTER ONE

The Spirit Guide Appears

Wind Dancer was lost. And frightened. Never before had she ventured so far from her village. Like the other Nez Percé girls and boys, she had been sent into the high meadows to dig for camas roots. And she'd done a good job, filling her basket to the brim.

But when New Arrows popped out of the grass and called, "You can't catch me, you're just a girl," Wind Dancer dropped everything and ran.

"You will take back your words, New Arrows," she cried, chasing after the boy on her strong brown legs.

Her long dark braids flew back over her shoulders. Wind Dancer felt the deep warmth of the late afternoon sun on her face. It was early spring. And

Wind Dancer felt as frisky as the young foals recently born to the mares in the Appaloosa herd.

The two friends raced through the tall grass.

"Your legs are like tree trunks," Wind Dancer shouted, gleefully leaping over a half-buried stump. "You won't have enough wind to beat me to the edge of the meadow."

Beyond the meadow loomed the forest of ponderosa pine and Douglas fir. All the children were under strict orders never to venture beyond the safety of the open meadow. Wind Dancer was sure New Arrows wouldn't run farther than the trees, and she was gaining on him with every step.

Only a few more paces, she thought, *and I've caught you.*

Suddenly New Arrows ducked into the dark gloom of the forest.

Wind Dancer tried to follow, but it was hard to see. The towering trees grew so close together that the rays of the sun barely penetrated to the forest floor. And after a few minutes, she was totally lost.

Wind Dancer stopped to listen. Surely a boy as boisterous as New Arrows would give himself away with the crack of a twig or a rustle in the brush. Nothing. No sound of him anywhere.

Wind Dancer closed her eyes and listened with

her heart, as her elders had taught her. She heard a sound. Of what?

Water! That's it. A stream is nearby. Maybe New Arrows is hiding there, using the water to cover his movements.

Wind Dancer crouched low and glided soundlessly through the forest on her moccasined feet.

At last she reached the stream and climbed onto a large gray boulder perched at the water's edge. Cupping her hands around her mouth, she called, "All right, New Arrows, you win. Come out and show yourself."

No answer.

"New Arrows? Didn't you hear me? I'm not playing this game anymore. You're the faster runner. I admit it."

Still no reply.

This was strange. Maybe New Arrows hadn't come this way at all. Maybe he'd circled back to the meadow and was hiding in the tall grass right now, giggling.

It would be just like him to play a trick like that, she thought. But where was the meadow?

Wind Dancer spun in a circle, trying to remember which direction she had come from. She prided herself on being one of the fastest runners in the tribe. And one of the best riders, too. But when it came to finding her way to some new place, or even an old place, she could get hopelessly lost.

Wind Dancer stood on her tiptoes trying to spot some sign—a broken branch, a deer trail—that would guide her back to her people in the meadow. The sun was dropping rapidly toward the horizon. Soon it would be nightfall.

Wind Dancer swallowed hard, trying to control the panic rising in her chest.

"I know I have been a foolish girl," she announced to the woods around her. "Many times I have ignored the counsel of my elders. But now I need help. I'm cold and hungry. I am afraid to stay alone in these woods. Please, somebody — anybody — help me find my way."

As if in answer, she heard a rustle in the leaves behind her.

Only half-daring to breathe, Wind Dancer turned to see who was there.

"Oh!" she gasped.

A magnificent spotted stallion stood quietly only a few feet away, his head lifted proudly. The horse's broad white back was dappled with dozens of black spots, which made him blend perfectly into the shadows of the rustling leaves.

Wind Dancer blinked her eyes. It was as if the

horse were a magical creature, shaped by the light and the wind.

This is no pack horse or old people's mount, Wind Dancer thought, trying to calm her racing pulse. *This is a buffalo hunter or war horse, for certain.*

Then the horse whinnied, a lilting phrase like a song. Wind Dancer knew she had never heard that melody before, yet it seemed very familiar, as if she'd always known it. Without thinking, she hummed the tune in response. To her delight the stallion tossed his head up and down.

He's talking to me, she thought. *To me!* She mustered her courage and said out loud, "Are you real? Or are you a ghost of the mountains?"

The horse snorted and took a few steps toward the woods. Then he stopped and looked back at her.

"Do—do you want me to follow you?" she asked, uncertainly.

The stallion whinnied again. Wind Dancer was confused. The horse was urging her to go in the opposite direction of where she was certain the meadow had to be. She was about to protest, but before she could say a word, the stallion reared up and batted his forelegs in the new direction.

He whinnied again, the same haunting tune as before, and Wind Dancer knew she had to trust him.

"I will follow where you lead," she said. "Take me home."

In answer the horse plunged into the forest undergrowth—and vanished.

"Wait!" Wind Dancer cried, running after him.

The brush was so thick that she couldn't see the horse at all. Only the drumming of his hooves and his distinctive whinny told her which way to go.

Suddenly the woods thinned out into a clearing, which opened to reveal a lush valley guarded by two mountains capped with snow. A silver thread of rippling water meandered through groves of cottonwoods and aspens, disappearing finally into the valley between the twin peaks.

"Yes," Wind Dancer murmured, gratefully. "This is the Wallowa Valley. This is my home."

From far away a familiar voice spoke, breaking into her dream. She opened her eyes.

"Jessie," her grandfather said gently. "We're ready to leave. It is time."

Hitting the Trail

66 I was dreaming," Jessie murmured, groggily. She opened one eye and peered around her. Gone were the beautiful meadow and river valley. In their place were the brown elkskin walls of her family's tipi.

She peered across the fire to where her mother and father usually slept. They had gone and taken their bedding with them.

"Oh, no!" Jessie sat up abruptly and threw back the heavy buffalo robes that covered her bedroll. "I overslept. They're going to leave without me!"

Her grandfather, who was dressed in a long range coat and black felt hat, laughed. "Calm down, little one," Gray Owl said. "We decided to let you sleep while your father packed the wagon."

Jessie wrapped a wool blanket around her shoulders and scurried across the hard-packed dirt floor of the tipi to get her traveling clothes. She shivered in the early morning cold. Spring in eastern Washington wasn't much warmer than winter. And on the Colville Reservation, the wind could get particularly fierce as it whipped across the hills.

"Grandfather, I had the strangest dream," she said, between chattering teeth. "It was more real to me than any I've ever had before."

"Tell me," he said. "Great wisdom often comes to us in our dreams."

"I was in a beautiful meadow, playing with New Arrows," Jessie said, brushing out her silky black hair that hung nearly to her waist. She plaited it carefully into two thick braids. "But I got lost. And I was so scared." Jessie paused, staring at the last embers glowing in the fire pit in the center of the tipi. "Then, just when I thought I'd never find my way home, a magnificent Appaloosa stallion appeared from out of nowhere. He bid me to follow him. And I did. To a land that was more beautiful than any country I have ever seen."

Gray Owl listened carefully to Jessie's dream. Then, in a voice that was almost a whisper, he said, "It seems that you have been visited by your *wayakin*."

"My *wayakin*?" Jessie repeated, with awe. *Wayakin* was the Nez Percé word for spirit guide. "But I haven't gone on a spirit quest."

In the old days, when a boy or girl reached ten or eleven years of age, they would be sent into the wilderness on a spirit quest. There they would fast for five days until they met their spirit guide. This guide would become their source of power and strength for the rest of their lives.

"No, you haven't gone on a spirit quest," Gray Owl said with a sigh. "Ever since our people were forced to leave our homeland, many of the old ways have been forgotten." A slow smile crept across his lips. "But perhaps not by the spirits."

"You mean since I didn't go find my *wayakin*, it has found me?" Jessie wondered.

"That is possible."

"But would my *wayakin* be a horse?" Jessie asked.

"Of course. It is the perfect choice." A chuckle rumbled deep in Gray Owl's chest. "You were riding horses before you could walk. While the other children clung to the manes of the old mares, you were riding the friskiest ponies. Now you join in the races, galloping faster and farther than almost anyone else in the tribe."

Jessie smiled proudly. That was why she had been called Wind Dancer. She'd always been proud of her Nez Percé name.

"Often the spirit guide will reveal a secret song or call. . ."

"His whinny!" Jessie cried. "It sounded like music."

Her grandfather nodded. "It's your *wayakin,* all right. Come to lead you to your new home."

Jessie shivered once more. But this time it wasn't from the cold. It was from excitement. A visit from her *wayakin.* At last!

"Now come and get some breakfast," Gray Owl said, moving to the entrance of the tipi. "There is much to do before we leave."

Just talking about breakfast made Jessie's stomach growl. Her mother and the other women of the tribe had probably already made some delicious biscuits at the cooking fire. "I'm coming," she called after her grandfather.

Jessie quickly slipped on her blue and white cotton blouse. Over that she pulled what Mrs. Webster, the Indian agent's wife, liked to call her angel dress. All of the women wore them.

Jessie's dress was light brown and made of heavy cotton with short sleeves that flared out at her elbows. The edges of the sleeves were trimmed in beautiful beadwork. She slipped her feet into the beaded elkskin moccasins that the women of her tribe had made especially for her.

She placed the traditional cone-shaped hat of the Nez Percé women on her head, then wrapped her brightly colored wool blanket around her shoulders. Jessie reached for her cornhusk bag where she kept her personal treasures and stepped through the door of the tipi. She was ready.

It was barely light out, but the entire tribe had risen to say good-bye to Jessie and her family. Some of the men were gathered by the wagon, their breath making puffs of mist in the chilly air. Most of the women and children huddled together around the cook fire.

Jessie hurried across the frost-covered ground, listening to the stiff grass crunch under her feet. She joined her mother, New Moon, at the fire and gratefully accepted two large biscuits.

As Jessie chewed her food, she took one last look at the place she had called home. Twelve tipis stood in a circle around the cook fire. That's where her people lived. Just outside the circle sat several log buildings. Beyond those was Captain Webster's gray-and-white home with its wide porch. Jessie knew that Captain Webster had been the Indian agent for their

reservation since before she was born.

Now Jessie's family was going away. The decision for them to leave had been difficult to reach. The tribal elders had spent many hours discussing it in council.

For the past five years, starting in 1906, her father, Red Wolf, had been training horses for the U.S. cavalry. The soldiers at the Colville Reservation counted on Red Wolf's expertise with horses, and particularly his skill with the beautiful spotted ones known as Appaloosas. When Red Wolf was offered work as a horse breeder at a ranch near Enterprise, Oregon, Jessie's grandfather had been overjoyed. Enterprise sat on the banks of the Wallowa River in the heart of their tribe's homeland, the Wallowa Valley.

The council knew it was important for the children of the Nez Percé to see the home of their ancestors, and they agreed that Red Wolf and his family should leave the rest of the tribe and go.

Jessie had been excited about her family's new adventure. But now that it was time to leave, she was sad and frightened. She had been born in the town of Nespelem on the Colville Reservation and had never known life outside the reservation.

Noticing her glum expression, New Moon said, "Come, let's walk. We can say our farewells, and when we return, it will be time to leave."

Jessie's friend New Arrows stood sadly by his family's tipi, waiting to say good-bye. When Jessie gave him the beaded belt she had sewn especially for him, she could hardly speak.

"Here," she said stiffly. "I'll miss you."

New Arrows nodded, unable to look her in the eye. His face was red, and she knew he was fighting back tears.

After Jessie said good-bye to her other friends, Annie Spring Leaf and Little Deer, it was time to say good-bye to her beloved Appaloosa.

Fleetfoot, his deep brown coat dotted with little white spots on the rump, was standing where he always stood each morning—right by the gate to the corral.

Fleetfoot saw her coming and eagerly pawed the ground.

Jessie dug in her bag, searching for the dried chokeberry cake she had set aside for this moment. She held it out to the horse and giggled as his muzzle tickled the palm of her hand.

Then she wrapped her arms around his neck and hugged him close. "I think I'm going to miss you most of all," she whispered, feeling hot tears well up in her eyes. "But we have too far to travel to bring you with us. Father says we have to take a steamboat, then two trains, and finally a wagon to get to the ranch. So you have to stay here."

Fleetfoot shook his short mane impatiently. Then he nudged her with his nose. Jessie felt as though her heart would burst. She buried her face in his mane, trying not to cry.

Finally her mother came to fetch her. Putting her hand on Jessie's shoulder, she murmured, "There will be many more horses where we are headed."

"I know that," Jessie said, wiping her eyes with the back of her sleeve. "But I already miss this one."

At that instant, Jessie heard a whinny like the one in her dream. Her eyes widened, and she turned toward the sound.

Puffs of gray smoke chugged along the horizon. It was the steamboat coming down the Columbia River. Coming to take them to a new life!

Suddenly Jessie was filled with new courage and hope. She hugged Fleetfoot one last time, then ran for the wagon.

"Farewell, Nespelem!" she cried to the bleak hills of the reservation. "Wallowa Valley—here we come!"

CHAPTER
THREE

Howdy, Harriet!

66"Hello!" A girl dressed in a navy-blue coat and high-buttoned shoes called to Jessie across the crowded train aisle. "My name's Harriet Elizabeth Johnson. What's yours?"

Jessie looked uncertainly at New Moon. She'd been instructed to sit quietly and not talk to strangers.

But they'd been traveling for two days. First on the steamboat down the Columbia River to Kennewick. Then on the Great Northern railroad to La Grande, where they'd switched to another line to take them to Enterprise, and their new home in the Wallowa Valley.

Jessie had been very good for most of the trip, not speaking to anyone, but she was eager to make friends. And here was a girl who looked just her age.

Luckily for Jessie, New Moon smiled and gave her permission with a nod. Her grandfather and father were dozing in the seat in front of them.

"My name's Jessie," she said, leaning across the aisle.

"Jessie?" The girl made a face. "That doesn't sound like an Indian name. Aren't you an Indian?"

Jessie nodded. "My Indian name is Wind Dancer, but my Christian name is Jessie."

Harriet had chubby cheeks and sparkling blue eyes. Her frizzy blond hair was gathered into a ponytail at her neck and tied with a wide blue ribbon. She grinned, revealing a big dimple in her left cheek. "Wind Dancer. I like that."

"Thank you," Jessie said. "I do, too."

Harriet turned to her mother, who was sitting beside the window, quietly sewing. "Mama, may I have an Indian name?" she asked. "Something pretty, like Soaring White Bird? Or Beautiful Pink Rose?"

Her mother was a plump woman in a maroon coat and matching hat with a big black plume. She looked up in surprise and blushed at her daughter's boldness. "I'm sorry, Harriet, but you can't," she whispered, tapping her daughter's knee. "Now don't bother that little girl."

"She's not bothering me," Jessie replied, leaning into the aisle to smile at Harriet's mother. "I like talking to her. And I'm not little, I'm ten years old."

"Why, so am I," Harriet said with a giggle. "Where are you going?"

Jessie proudly announced, "My father has a new job on the biggest ranch in the Wallowa Valley."

"Really!" Harriet's blue eyes widened. "You mean the Macintire Ranch?"

Jessie nodded excitedly.

"That's where *we* live!" Harriet turned and tugged at her mother's sleeve. "Mama, did you hear that? Jessie's father is coming to work on the ranch."

Harriet's mother smiled at Jessie and introduced herself to Jessie's mother. "I'm Mrs. Johnson. I cook for the Macintires."

"And I help out with chores," Harriet said. She wrinkled her nose. "Sometimes it can be a lot of hard work. Especially during calving season in the spring, and haying in the fall. And up until now, I was the only girl on the ranch, so I didn't have any friends."

Jessie frowned. "There aren't any other children on the ranch?"

"Well, there's Gus. He just turned eleven." She lowered her voice and confided, "Gus can be bossy sometimes, just because his pa's the ranch foreman."

"Is he the only other child in the valley?"

"Oh, no!" Harriet giggled. "There are twenty-three children in our school alone."

Jessie felt a shiver run up her arms. Twenty-three! That seemed like a lot.

Harriet pointed to an empty wooden seat near the rear of the car. "Let's go back there, so we can really talk."

Jessie skipped down the aisle with Harriet to the back of the train car. The two girls scooted down low in the seat, so just the top of Jessie's hat and Harriet's bow could be seen from the front.

"Mama hates to ride on trains," Harriet confided. "The rocking motion makes her woozy. But I love it."

"You've ridden on a train before?" Jessie was impressed.

Harriet nodded. "Lots of times. When my pa died, we took a really long train trip, all the way from Illinois. Now we go to Spokane once a year to see Mama's sister, Aunt Martha, and to do shopping for the ranch."

Jessie liked the way Harriet said, *the ranch*. As if she owned it. Soon she'd be talking that way, too.

"What's your pa going to do on the ranch?" Harriet asked, digging in her coat pocket for a stick of horehound candy. She broke the stick in two and handed a piece to Jessie.

"He'll help Mr. Macintire—"

"*Colonel* Macintire," Harriet corrected. "He was with President Roosevelt in the Spanish-American war, and is extremely proud of it."

Jessie nodded. "*Colonel* Macintire. My father's going to help him breed Appaloosas." She took a lick of the sweet candy.

"I like the ones that are completely covered in spots from head to toe. The Colonel calls them leopard spots." Harriet crunched into her brown candy stick.

"For over a hundred years my people have bred Appaloosas," Jessie declared proudly. "We made the Appaloosa the best horse on the plains."

Whoo-ooh!

The steam whistle blew at the head of the train. Then the conductor entered the car and called loudly, "Next stop, Enterprise, Oh-ree-gone." Both girls sat up expectantly.

Jessie's window had fogged up from the warmth of the passengers crowding the car. Using the back of her fist, she rubbed on the glass until she'd cleared a small circle.

When she peered outside, she gasped with surprise. There, ringed by snowcapped mountains was the valley from her dream. A stream rambled through the heart of it, and off in the distance she could just see the glint of a crystal blue lake.

"Grandfather!" Jessie cried.

Gray Owl hurried back to meet her. "What is it, child? Is something the matter?"

Jessie pointed to the window. "This valley. Those mountains. The stream." The words tumbled out of Jessie's mouth in a rush. "I've seen them before. In my dream."

Gray Owl nodded. "I am not surprised. It is here, in this valley, that the *Nimipu* were born. And in those meadows the first Appaloosas were bred."

The tiny hairs on the back of Jessie's neck stood up. Gray Owl had used the Indian name for their tribe, *Nimipu*. It meant "the Real People." Jessie's voice was barely a whisper as she asked, "Then this is our home?"

For the first time in Jessie's life, she saw her grandfather's eyes brim with tears. "Yes, Wind Dancer." He raised his chin proudly. "This is our home."

Queen of the Appaloosas

"Yeow!" Harriet cried as the wagon bounced over yet another hole in the road. "That one hurt, Rusty!"

"Quit your complainin', Harriet," Rusty shouted from his perch on the driver's seat of the wagon. The lanky ranchhand had been sent to pick them up at the train station. "Or I'll make you come up here and take Midge and Bessie's reins."

"He'd never let me drive the wagon," Harriet whispered to Jessie. "He's just fooling."

Jessie was glad. The wagon was loaded to the brim, and she could see that Midge and Bessie, the two black Clydesdales, were straining to get up some of the hills. It was going to take an experienced hand at the reins to get them to the ranch.

Jessie's father, Red Wolf, sat beside Rusty on the driver's bench up front. Mrs. Johnson, New Moon, and Gray Owl were crowded into the seat behind them. Jessie and Harriet had wedged themselves in with the luggage and crates of supplies.

After leaving the depot, the wagon quickly left the town behind, and soon they were rumbling past acres of open pasture. Unlike the drab hills of Nespelem, spring was in full bloom in the Wallowa Valley. The meadows were green and lush, with purple shooting stars, bluebells, pink bitterroots, and yellow sunflowers beginning to bloom.

"Will we be there soon?" Jessie asked.

In half an hour, they had only passed one small farm. Jessie was eager to catch her first glimpse of the ranch and kept craning her neck around to watch for it.

"Here we are," Rusty called as the wagon bounced through an open gate. "We've just entered the Macintire Ranch."

Thick posts on either side of the road marked the ends of two long stretches of barbed wire fence that stretched across the valley in opposite directions until they disappeared from view.

"But I don't even see a house or anything," Jessie cried in dismay.

"It's a big ranch. We won't see the house for another twenty or so minutes," Rusty replied.

"It's *that* big?" Jessie gasped.

Rusty pointed off to the ridge of mountains rimming the valley to the southeast. "See that peak jutting up over there? That's Eagle Cap. The property runs all the way up the side of that mountain. And over there. . . ." He shifted position and pointed to the west. "It goes pretty near to the bottom of Mount Fanny."

"You mean Colonel Macintire owns this entire valley?" Jessie gasped.

"He's a very rich man," Harriet replied in a respectful whisper.

"I remember a time," Gray Owl said quietly, "a time when our people lived here. I was a boy."

Harriet turned to Jessie and whispered, "Your grandfather lived here?"

Jessie nodded. "With Chief Joseph. But Grandfather doesn't like to talk about it."

"Why?"

"It's a sad story," Jessie said. "For a long time our people lived in peace with the ranchers in this valley. But one day a prospector found gold in the mountains.

Suddenly strangers poured in from everywhere. They wanted our land. My people refused to give it up. The government had promised us it would be ours forever."

"But some men have short memories," Gray Owl said, never taking his eyes off the hills around them.

"So the treaty was broken?" Harriet asked.

Jessie nodded. "The army tried to force the Nez Percé to move to a reservation in Idaho. Some did, but not Chief Joseph. He rounded up his band, and a great herd of Appaloosas, and all of them fled to Canada."

"Was your grandfather with them?"

Jessie nodded. "It was a terrible time. The elders tell us the tribe lost nine hundred horses just trying to cross the Salmon River. They ran for over a thousand miles, fighting off the army the whole way. But it was winter and the people were cold and starving. Children were dying."

"How terrible," Harriet murmured.

"So Chief Joseph surrendered. He went to speak with General Howard himself, and said. . ."

Jessie's grandfather closed his eyes and repeated the great chief's famous words: "From where the sun now stands, I will fight no more forever."

After Gray Owl finished speaking, Jessie and Harriet rode in silence for awhile. Jessie looked out at the rich pastures and hillsides and tried to imagine her people living in this valley. The women and girls would be scattered across the meadows, gathering camas roots and wild berries. She noticed an outcropping of boulders and pictured the boys scrambling over it, playing at war games. The men would be tending their great herds of Appaloosa horses.

The thundering of hoofbeats cut into Jessie's daydream. At first she thought the sound was in her imagination. Then she sat up and peered over the side of the wagon.

Dozens of horses were running together on the other side of the fence. There were chestnuts, sorrels, and bays, and mixed in among the herd were a few spotted ones. They thundered along the fence, tossing their manes.

As the herd angled back to the center of the field, one horse remained. A beautiful Appaloosa mare. Her mane and tail matched her rich chestnut coat. Brown specks dappled her white rump. She paused by the fence, with her majestic head held high.

"Look at *that* one," Harriet cried. "She looks like she's posing to have her picture painted."

"She looks so proud, like a beautiful star," Jessie announced.

"Funny you should say that," Rusty called over his

shoulder. "Her name is Morning Star. Before the Colonel bought her, she belonged to a trick rider in one of the Wild West shows. She sure acts like a star, too. She won't have a thing to do with the other horses."

"The mare will be foaling soon," Jessie's father pointed out. "Maybe that's why she keeps to herself."

"Nope." Rusty shook his head decisively. "Morning Star's always been that way. A regular queen of the Appaloosas."

As if responding to the cowhand's words, Morning Star tossed her head and whinnied. Then, in a flash, she galloped over the small rise in front of them and disappeared.

"I like her spirit," Jessie said, smiling.

The wagon lumbered up the low hill and, as they crested the top, Harriet cried, "There's the ranch."

"I see it!" Jessie gasped. "It's enormous!"

The road ran down the hill through another fenced gate, then curved up to the front of a splendid two-story, white-frame house. The porch lining the entire front of the house was supported by four large white columns. A carefully manicured lawn with two big beautiful oak trees framed the house. Jessie had never seen anything so grand in her life.

"Mrs. Macintire had that house built to look just

like her old home back in Virginia," Rusty explained.

"We live next to the bunkhouse," Harriet said. "It's that long white building behind the main house." She turned back to Jessie. "You'll probably live over there, too."

A horseshoe-shaped drive wrapping around the main house was lined with buildings. Two huge red barns sat side by side, connected by a large corral.

"We store all of the farm equipment in the south barn," Rusty said. "The main barn stables the animals. The bunkhouse, where me and the other ranchhands live, is next to the main barn. Then there's a bunch of houses bordering the length of the back pasture. That's where Charlie Shaw, the ranch foreman, and his family live. Plus Mrs. Macintire's brother's got himself a small house there, too."

"Small?" Jessie repeated. Nothing looked small on this ranch. Everything seemed huge. There were horse barns and cattle barns, chicken coops and work sheds and smokehouses. It looked like a whole town.

As Rusty guided the wagon into the yard, another ranchhand came running from the barn, waving his hat. "Stop, Rusty. Pull up!"

"Whoa, there," Rusty said, pulling back on the reins. "What's wrong, Tom?"

Tom bent over to catch his breath. "Smokey—the

stallion—he jumped the fence to get in with the mares. And he's cut himself on the wire."

"Where's Charlie and the Colonel?" Rusty asked.

"They took most of the boys out to Top Hat for spring calving," Tom replied. "It's just me and Tulsa."

"Hold on one sec, and I'll help ya." Rusty turned to Jessie's father, but Red Wolf was already out of the wagon. His leather bag of medical supplies was looped over his shoulder.

"I'll help, too," Red Wolf told Tom.

"Then follow me." Tom started to run toward the pasture, but Red Wolf stopped him.

"Wait. First send this fellow Tulsa to get the boss."

The authority in Red Wolf's voice was so clear that Tom nodded immediately.

"Then you two corral the mares," Red Wolf told Tom and Rusty. He glanced toward the pasture and said, "I will take care of the stallion."

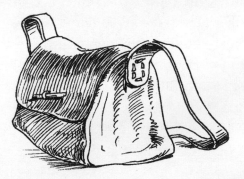

CHAPTER
FIVE

Red Wolf to the Rescue

Jessie and Harriet sprinted toward the pasture. The stallion, a magnificent dark-brown horse covered with hundreds of tiny white spots, was snorting and running wild-eyed around the fenced enclosure. About twenty frightened mares were circling and wheeling to keep out of his way.

Red Wolf had now entered the pasture. While Rusty and Tom shooed the mares into the far corner, waving their hands and whooping, the stallion zigzagged from one side to the other. As Smokey ran, they could see the gash on his side.

"That's got to hurt," Harriet said, wincing for the horse.

Jessie didn't reply. She was too busy worrying about her father. Red Wolf had been hired to care for the Appaloosas. If he couldn't take care of this one, then his job might be finished before it began.

She held her breath as her father walked slowly and calmly to the center of the grassy field. He wasn't carrying a bridle or even a rope. Smokey noticed him and hesitated, cocking his head.

Red Wolf faced the stallion and locked eyes with the big horse. Then he began to talk in a rhythmic chant.

"What's he doing?" Harriet whispered.

"My father's speaking to Smokey in our language," Jessie whispered back. "He's letting the horse know they are kin."

Smokey had stopped his skittering around the field. His ears were flattened back against his head. Then one ear pricked forward, listening. And then the other. Finally the stallion lowered his head.

"What's your father saying now?" Harriet whispered.

"He's singing to the horse. He's telling Smokey he respects him. That we are all creatures of this earth, and we need to help each other when we are hurt."

Red Wolf walked forward, one step at a time, never stopping his chant, until he was an arm's length

from Smokey's shoulder. Slowly he ran his hands up
Smokey's coat until they rested on his withers. They
stood that way for several minutes. Then Red Wolf slid
his hand forward and took hold of Smokey's mane.
With a gentle tug, he led the horse over to the rail,
where Tom was waiting with a halter. Jessie's mother
and grandfather stood nearby.

Red Wolf smoothly slipped the halter onto the
stallion and led him into the barn, with everyone but
the cowhands following behind. The great horse
snorted once or twice but stayed calm. Inside the
barn, Red Wolf tied Smokey's lead rope to a sturdy
post. Finally Red Wolf looked at Gray Owl and nodded.

"What's happening now?" Harriet asked.

"He wants Grandfather to bring him his medicine
bag," Jessie explained. "He's going to stitch up the
cut."

"Ew!" Harriet wrinkled her nose. "I can't look."

Jessie cocked her head and grinned. "It isn't as
bad as you think, Harriet. The cut isn't that deep. And
once Father makes a poultice and applies it to the
wound, Smokey will hardly feel the stitches."

The girls watched Red Wolf and New Moon make
a paste to smear on the horse's side.

"Yuck," Harriet muttered. "That stuff looks awful."

"It's made of pine tar, willow bark, and comfrey,"

Jessie told her friend. "It's good for the horse. He'll heal in no time."

Once the poultice had been applied, Red Wolf threaded his needle. While he worked on Smokey, he kept up his chant.

The horse stood quietly, not even flinching as Red Wolf took some stitches to close his cut.

All at once Rusty, who'd come in to watch Red Wolf work, sprang to attention.

"Colonel Macintire's back," he hissed out of the corner of his mouth.

Jessie looked out the barn and saw two riders pounding up the drive at a full gallop. One of them was Tulsa. The other was clearly Colonel Macintire.

The Colonel looked like a picture that Jessie had once seen of Buffalo Bill, the famous showman who had toured his Wild West Show all over the world. With his white handlebar mustache and bushy white eyebrows, the Colonel cut an imposing figure. Perched on his head was a broad-brimmed cowboy hat.

Colonel Macintire leapt off his horse, handing Tulsa the reins. Then he strode toward them and announced in a booming voice, "Tulsa told me about the problem. Let's take a look."

The Colonel hunkered down beside Red Wolf to examine the wound. Jessie's father was just finishing his work on Smokey's belly and didn't even look up. His total concentration was on taking care of the horse.

Jessie joined her grandfather and mother, who stood a respectful distance from Colonel Macintire, waiting for him to acknowledge them. In her tribe, the elders always did the talking. And no one ever spoke until they were invited to speak.

Jessie stared at the ground, afraid to even raise her head to look at this huge man who would be their boss.

After he had inspected Red Wolf's handiwork, the Colonel straightened up and, removing his hat, introduced himself to the family. He shook each of their hands, starting with Gray Owl, and boomed a hearty, "Welcome to the ranch."

Jessie was so nervous that she couldn't speak. She could only smile shyly.

The Colonel nodded to Harriet and her mother. "Good to have you back, Mrs. Johnson. The boys have been whinin' and moanin' the whole time you were away. Seems no one else can bake an apple pie the way you can."

Harriet smiled at her mother, who blushed with pleasure.

Colonel Macintire turned to Red Wolf. "That

stallion cost me a pretty penny and truth to tell, I wasn't ready to see that money go up in smoke." He shook Red Wolf's hand and clapped him on the shoulder. "You've done a mighty fine job, Red Wolf. I'm glad you and your family have joined us on the Macintire Ranch."

Although Red Wolf only murmured his thanks, Jessie could see the pride shining in her father's eyes. And for the moment, she let her fear of these strange new surroundings and this tall white man with the thundering voice subside. Her heart was full.

CHAPTER
SIX

The Wayakin Returns

66L**ight," Jessie murmured a few days later. "Where's that light coming from?"

She opened her eyes and stared up. This was odd. Her eyes were not seeing the smooth leather hides of her family's tipi but rather the flat boards of a wooden ceiling. Daylight streamed in through a glass window on the south wall of the little clapboard house.

Jessie sat up in alarm, clutching the sides of her bed. Then she forced herself to take a deep breath and relax. She'd been at the ranch for three days, but she still wasn't used to sleeping on a bed so far from the ground. Jessie was afraid she might have a nightmare and fall onto the hard wooden floor.

"Well, you're up at last," her mother called out from her place in front of the wood stove.

"Did I oversleep?" Jessie asked, rubbing her eyes with her fists. She'd had a fitful night, tossing and turning on this strange mattress in this odd house with its thick walls.

In Nespelem, Jessie had lulled herself to sleep on her bedroll of buffalo robes, listening to the wind rustle softly in the trees outside the tipi. But here, all the comforting night sounds were shut out by the wooden walls.

"This is a big day for you," New Moon said, putting a kettle of water to boil on the wood stove. "Your first day of school."

"School!" Just saying the word sent a tremor of fear rippling through Jessie's insides. "So soon? Couldn't I wait another day or two?"

"And what will you do while I'm at work?" New Moon replied, laying a cream-colored blouse, navy-blue jumper, and wool leggings at the foot of Jessie's bed.

"I'll help you," Jessie said. "Just like Harriet helps her mother."

"Harriet's going to school, too." New Moon wrapped her coat around her shoulders, and headed for the front door. "Now you hurry and get dressed."

"Where are you going?" Jessie asked.

"I'm taking your father some hot coffee. He's already had his breakfast and has gone to check on the stallion. Grandfather's helping him change the bandage."

The front door closed with a click and her mother was gone. Suddenly Jessie felt terribly lonely and frightened. "I won't know anyone," she murmured, slipping on her muslin blouse and wool jumper. Over that she tied a print apron. "And they'll think I'm ugly. I just know it."

Jessie padded over to the small cracked mirror hanging over the wooden sideboard in the front room and stared at her reflection. A caramel-skinned girl with deep brown eyes shaped like almonds, and a long, thin nose stared back at her. "How will I ever fit in?" she asked herself.

As if in answer to her question, a whinny sounded from the side pasture. The same strange call she'd heard in her dream the day she left Nespelem.

Jessie hurriedly rebraided her hair, then slipped her feet into her leather moccasins and grabbed her wool blanket coat and cornhusk bag. Luckily, her mother had left a tray of biscuits sitting on the small table in front of the stove. Jessie grabbed a couple and bolted out the front door.

When she reached the pasture fence, Jessie stood still and gasped.

Standing in the distance was Morning Star, the beautiful mare she had seen the day they arrived at the ranch. But next to Morning Star, shrouded in the early morning mist, was the horse from Jessie's dream. She was certain of it. He was a snow-white stallion dappled with black oval-shaped spots, with a black mane and tail.

Jessie didn't even hesitate. In a moment she was over the fence and pounding through the wet grass toward the pair of horses. But by the time she reached the mare's side, the other horse—the magnificent stallion from her dream—had vanished.

Jessie was disappointed but not for long. Morning Star bent down her long neck and gently nuzzled Jessie's cheek with her muzzle. Morning Star's nose felt as soft as velvet.

"You saw him, didn't you, Morning Star?" Jessie asked, reaching up and scratching the mare behind the ear. "Was that my *wayakin*? My spirit guide, come to help me start a new life on this ranch?"

Morning Star puffed warm breath through her nostrils and nudged Jessie's shoulder with her head.

"What are you trying to tell me?" Jessie giggled. "That he's not my spirit guide, but your secret love?"

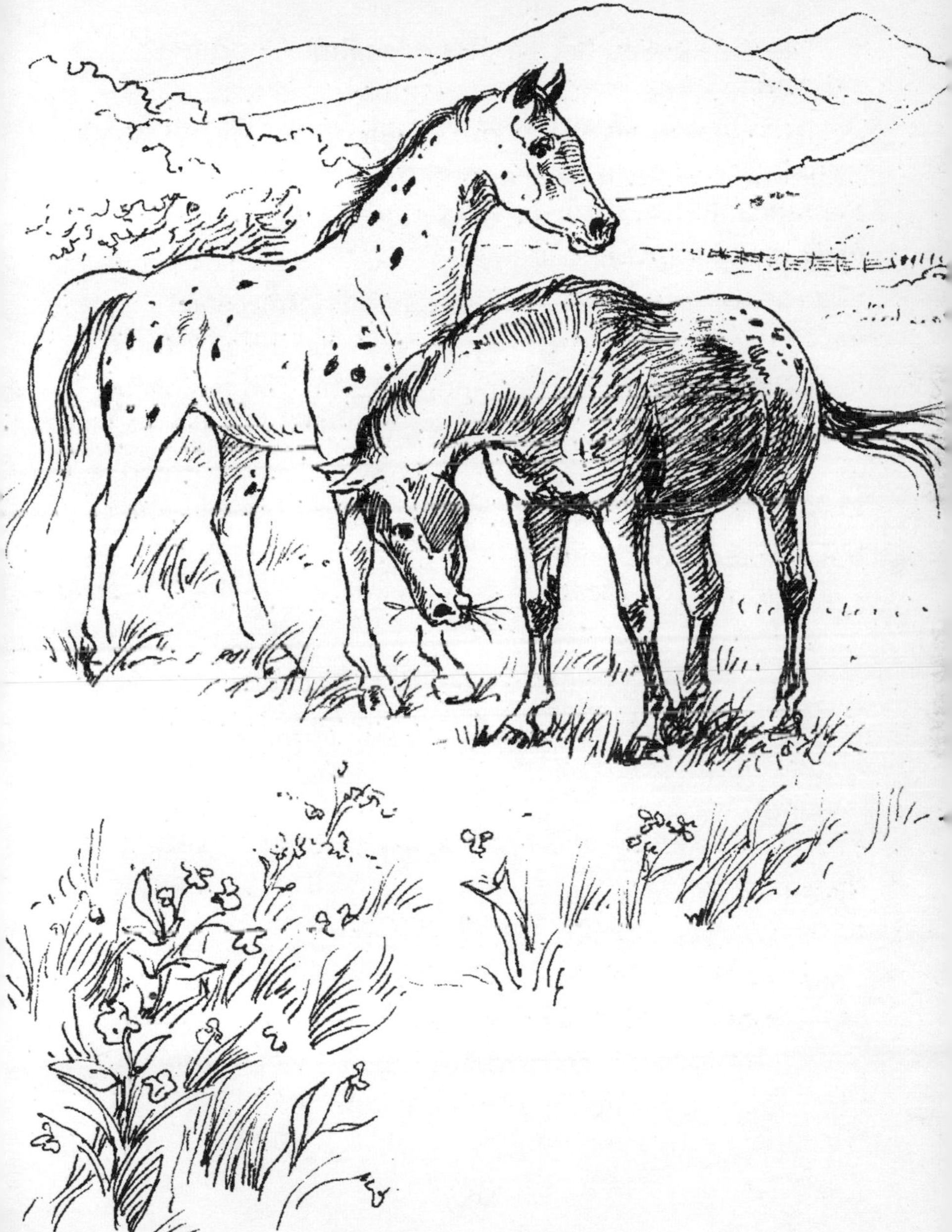

Jessie stroked her hand the length of Morning Star's neck, down across her withers, and gently patted her side. "You are the queen of the Appaloosas. And soon you will have your little prince or princess."

"Yoo-hoo!" a voice called from the fence. "Jessie! It's time for school!"

It was Harriet. She sported two enormous red bows, one around each pigtail. She held a book and small blackboard in one hand and a tin lard pail in the other. "Mother packed us both a lunch."

Jessie wrapped her arms tightly around Morning Star's neck. "Today's my first day of school," she murmured. "Wish me luck!"

Morning Star replied with several loud snorts and a whinny.

Jessie ran to join her friend. But this time when she climbed over the fence, the hem of her jumper snagged the fence rail, and they heard a loud ripping sound.

"Oh, no!" Jessie gasped. "That's my best jumper. I've torn it."

"You'll have to fix it later." Harriet was already backing down the road. "We don't want to be tardy. Miss Quimby hates latecomers!"

Jessie swallowed hard. It would be just her luck to arrive late for school with torn clothes and have Miss

Quimby get mad at her.

"Well, come on, then," she shouted, catching hold of Harriet's elbow and dragging her down the lane. "Let's run!"

CHAPTER SEVEN

Trouble at Sunnyside School

When Jessie and Harriet crested the hill by Sunnyside School, the big brass bell was already ringing, signaling that class was about to start. Several older boys were racing across the yard toward the trim white-frame building.

Jessie could feel her heart thudding in her chest as she and Harriet crossed the threshold to the one-room schoolhouse. Once inside the narrow entryway, Jessie took off her coat and hung it on a wooden peg next to Harriet's.

Jessie took a deep breath and stepped into the classroom. To her left was a shelf with a bucket of water and a tin dipper. A wood stove sat in the back corner, some split wood stacked neatly beside it. Four rows of wooden desks faced the worn blackboard. They were filled with children ranging in age from six to fourteen.

At the head of the class sat a heavy oak desk and chair. A young woman whose hair was pulled into a tight bun stood at the blackboard with her back to them.

"That's Miss Quimby," Harriet whispered to Jessie. "She's our schoolmarm."

Miss Quimby was writing out the day's assignment in chalk. She was very tall, with a long face, and a sharp, long nose. Even the fingers on her hands seemed to be extra long and thin. A pair of gold-rimmed glasses pinched the tip of her nose.

The teacher spotted Harriet and Jessie hovering at the back of the room. She waved her eraser at them. "I see we have our new student. Harriet, why don't you introduce your friend to the class?"

All twenty-two boys and girls in the class turned to stare. Harriet, who was clearly nervous about speaking in front of the group, gestured shyly to her new friend. "This is Jessie. She just moved here. Her father's working on the Macintire Ranch."

Miss Quimby folded her hands in front of her and smiled at Jessie. "And where are you from, Jessie?"

"Nespelem, Washington," Jessie replied, with a shy smile at her teacher.

"That's on the Colville Reservation," Harriet explained. "Jessie's a Nez Percé Indian."

"Nez Percé," a beefy boy in bib overalls and a plaid shirt repeated. "Say, aren't you that tribe that wears rings in your noses?"

Everyone in the room laughed, and Jessie felt her face instantly heat up. "That's not true!" she cried.

Miss Quimby adjusted her glasses and peered at the boy. "Floyd, they don't wear rings now."

"That's right," Jessie said, raising her chin indignantly. "We've never worn nose rings."

Miss Quimby lifted one finger. "It's my understanding that your people did wear decorations in your noses. That's how your tribe got its name." She closed her eyes and tapped her forehead. "As I recall, about a hundred years ago French trappers saw some native women in these parts wearing shells in their noses, so they called the tribe the Nez Percé, which in French means pierced nose."

All at once it seemed as if every child in the classroom was staring at Jessie's nose, looking for the hole where a ring should go. Jessie covered her nose with her hand self-consciously. "Um, excuse me, Miss Quimby, but I was taught that that story is all wrong."

Miss Quimby raised an eyebrow. "Oh? And what did you hear?"

"Well. . ." Jessie cleared her throat and moved a few feet away from the potbellied stove. It was making her start to sweat. "I was taught that a trapper met one of my ancestors and asked his guide what kind of people we were. The guide answered in sign language by moving his finger from left to right under his nose. Like this." Jessie demonstrated.

"And what does that mean?" Miss Quimby asked.

Jessie answered proudly. "It means 'brave under fire.'"

"Hah!" one of the boys whispered. "Some brave people. The first sign of a white man in this valley, and they ran like rabbits."

Jessie was standing close enough to overhear the boy and anger surged through her. "That's not true," she shouted. "My people were pushed out by greedy men who wanted our land."

Miss Quimby's eyes widened behind her glasses. "Shouting will not be tolerated in this classroom, young lady."

Jessie's face was already hot from the potbellied stove, but now her cheeks blazed a deep red. She stared down at the wooden floor and murmured, "I'm sorry, Miss Quimby."

"Apology accepted," Miss Quimby replied. She turned to Harriet. "After we do the flag salute and prayer, will you help Jessie find an empty desk?"

"Yes, ma'am," Harriet said.

Miss Quimby smiled primly. "Good. Now class, will everyone please rise."

The class faced the faded American flag in the corner and placed their hands over their hearts. As everyone around her murmured the pledge of allegiance, Jessie remained silent. She was too embarrassed to talk.

After the prayer, Harriet looped her arm through Jessie's. "Don't be upset," she whispered. "That boy Floyd Perkins is a big bully. He gets everyone in trouble. Now come on, let's get you situated."

Jessie pulled back. "Maybe I should just stay here, in the back."

"Don't be silly," Harriet hissed. "If you sit by that wood stove, you'll melt. And if you sit up front by my desk, you'll freeze like I do. Look, here's a desk in the middle, far away from mean ol' Floyd Perkins."

"Thanks," Jessie murmured gratefully as she slid into her desk. Her ears were still burning with humiliation. Miss Quimby passed her a worn *McGuffey's Reader*, which she carefully placed in front of her beside her writing tablet and pencil. Then Jessie sat miserably with her hands folded and her eyes downcast.

What a terrible beginning!

Jessie the Ranch Girl

The rest of the school day went by in a dreary blur. Jessie barely heard the teacher's lessons. The lunch Mrs. Johnson had prepared for Harriet and Jessie consisted of a couple of thick slices of freshly baked bread, two hunks of jack cheese, and an apple apiece. Normally, Jessie would have devoured it hungrily, but the morning's humiliation had made her lose her appetite.

When two o'clock finally came and Miss Quimby dismissed the class, Jessie breathed a huge sigh of relief. She just wanted to go home.

"Let's walk with the Carter girls," Harriet suggested, as they slipped on their coats in the entryway. "They're from the Double K ranch, next to ours."

They hurried to catch up with Cora and Fannie Carter, who were talking excitedly about an upcoming barn dance. In their matching yellow gingham dresses the Carter girls looked like twins, even though Cora, at twelve, was a full year and a half younger than Fannie. Both sisters had the same cornsilk blond hair and sprinkle of freckles across their noses.

"The Barclays said that everyone from Pendleton to Grangeville is invited," Fannie was saying. "It's going to be as big a shindig as the Reynolds barn raising last May."

"Who's going to play?" Harriet asked. "Your pa and the Cleary brothers?"

"Oh, no," Fannie replied. "The band is coming all the way from Portland."

Harriet whistled low under her breath. "That should be something."

"I just love dances," Cora gushed. Then she looked at Jessie and covered her mouth. "I'm sorry. You probably don't know about these things, growing up on a reservation and all."

Jessie cocked her head in confusion. "My tribe has dances."

"But not like civilized people," Fannie pointed out.

"A dance with a band and partners."

"That's not a very nice thing to say," Harriet cut in. "I'll bet those tribal dances are just as civilized as ours. I remember at our last dance, Tucker Reynolds' pa had too much punch and upchucked right in the middle of the dance floor." She rolled her eyes. "Do you call that civilized?"

"Well, of course not," Cora replied, with a toss of her long blond braid. "But I thought Indians wore a lot of feathers and hopped around campfires, whooping and yelling."

"They do more than that." Harriet gave Jessie a nudge with her elbow. "Tell 'em."

"It's true we do have our traditional dances," Jessie explained, tentatively. "And that's when we wear our finest dresses. They're usually covered with lots of beautiful beadwork. And the men wear eagle-feather headdresses."

"See?" Cora said to Harriet. "They do wear feathers."

"But there are other things that go on," Jessie added. "For instance, the stick game."

"The stick game?" Fannie scrunched up her face. "What's that?"

"The elders play it," Jessie said. "While many men drum, a stick is passed around a circle, and one person has to guess where it is."

"That's it?" Cora asked.

Jessie nodded. "It can go on for hours and hours."

"Sounds kind of silly," Fannie murmured.

Jessie started to protest but quickly shut her mouth. The stick game was one of her grandfather's favorite pastimes, and taken very seriously by everyone in her tribe. But now that she thought about it, she could see how white people could probably find it a pretty silly game. And dancing in long feathered headdresses wearing masks of birds and animals would probably seem odd to them, too.

The girls reached the fork in the road and the Carter sisters said good-bye. Jessie tried to smile and wave cheerily, but she felt as if a dark cloud had settled across her heart.

"Ignore them," Harriet said, with a wave of the hand. "They didn't mean to hurt your feelings. They just don't know any better."

The girls trudged the rest of the long road home. But as they came over the hill above the ranch, the cloud over Jessie's heart seemed to lift. Out prancing in the pasture, looking as beautiful and sassy as ever, was Morning Star.

The spotted horse shook her proud head and whinnied.

"I think she's happy to see us," Jessie said with a chuckle. "And I sure am happy to see her!"

Jessie ducked her head and ran as fast as her legs would carry her over to the fence. "Guess what I brought you!" Jessie called to the mare as she dug in her coat pocket looking for the treat she'd saved from lunch. "A nice, shiny red apple."

Morning Star took the entire apple in one bite, and chewed with her muzzle still pressed into Jessie's palm.

"You sure like horses." Harriet bent over to catch her breath. She had raced to keep up with Jessie but had gotten a stitch in her side halfway to the fence.

"I love them," Jessie murmured, nuzzling her face into Morning Star's mane. "My people always have. Especially the beautiful Appaloosa."

"The Carter family loves Appaloosas, too," Harriet said. "I wonder how they'd feel if they knew that your people practically invented them."

Jessie smiled. "We didn't invent the Appaloosa. We just figured out how to breed them. And now my father will pass that skill on to the people of this ranch."

Jessie quietly stroked Morning Star's neck.

"What are you thinking about, Jessie?" Harriet finally asked. "You look sad."

"I was thinking that my people have always been able to change their ways to fit the times. We used to be salmon fishers, but when we discovered the horse, we soon became buffalo hunters. And wanderers. Each place our tribe was forced to go—from the horrible hot plains of Oklahoma to the freezing cold hills of eastern Washington—we learned to adjust." Jessie raised her head to look at the Macintire mansion with its big white pillars and sweeping porch. "And now I must adjust, too."

Harriet looked puzzled. "What do you mean?"

"Well, I have to face the fact that I live on a modern ranch now," Jessie explained. "Not a reservation. I don't sleep on the ground in a tipi made of skins. I've got my own bed in a house built of wood."

"So?"

"It's time to forget about being a Nez Percé. I need to concentrate on being a ranch girl."

Morning Star seemed to have a different opinion and butted Jessie with her head. Jessie stumbled backwards. "Stop that, Morning Star," she complained. "This is serious."

"But how are you going to become a ranch girl?" Harriet asked.

Jessie kicked one foot in the air. "I'll start by

getting rid of these moccasins. I should wear boots, like all the other girls at Sunnyside School."

Harriet seemed concerned about Jessie's change of heart. "Are you sure about this?"

Jessie nodded firmly. "I'm positive."

"Um, if you're really serious," Harriet said tentatively, "I have an old pair of boots you could borrow, but they may be a little small."

Jessie's eyes lit up. "That doesn't matter. Oh, thank you, Harriet."

On the way back to her house, Jessie stopped at Harriet's cabin to borrow the boots. They were made of stiff black leather with at least twenty buttons up the sides. Harriet dug in her trunk and pulled out a strange-looking piece of metal with a loop at one end and a little crook at the other. "You're going to need this. It's a buttonhook."

When Jessie returned to her room that evening, she carefully removed her moccasins and wrapped them in a piece of flannel. Then she tucked her beautiful cornhusk purse and the beaded moccasins away in the bottom of her trunk.

"From this moment on," Jessie said, shutting the trunk lid firmly, "I am no longer Wind Dancer of the *Nimipu*, but Jessie the ranch girl."

A Prince Is Born

"Wake up, little one," Gray Owl said.
"Wake up!"

Jessie rolled over. It was still dark outside. Too
early to get up.

But the oil lamps had been lit in the front room,
and she saw several figures rushing about in the
kitchen.

"What's the matter?" Jessie cried, as she sat up
and wrapped the wool blanket around her shoulders.
"Is there a fire?"

Fire was the one thing that sent fear into the
hearts of everyone at the ranch.

"No," her grandfather chuckled. "Morning Star's

giving birth. I thought you'd want to be there to help."

That woke Jessie up in a hurry. She had been looking forward to this moment, and now it was finally here. "Oh, thank you, Grandfather. I wouldn't miss it for the world."

A month had passed since Jessie and her family had arrived at the Macintire Ranch. In that time, Jessie had watched Morning Star go from being slightly heavy with foal to huge. For the past few days, her belly had looked as though it were ready to burst. The whole ranch had been on call, waiting for the birth of Morning Star's foal.

"The mare's water has broken," her mother reported.

"Is she still on her feet?" Jessie asked, scurrying around in the dim light, trying to get dressed. She hastily pulled her wool dress over her nightgown. Then she dug in her trunk for a pair of stockings and pulled on the high-button boots she had borrowed from Harriet.

"She's lying down in the straw," New Moon replied. "And they just got a glimpse of the birth sac."

Jessie's heart thudded a little faster. She knew what that meant. Morning Star was getting ready to push out her foal. "We'd better hurry," she cried.

Her grandfather held the lantern aloft as they

hurried across the yard toward the barn with the stables. Even though it was April, the nights were still chilly in the Wallowa Valley. Jessie puffed out little clouds of smoke in the yellow lantern light.

The boots Harriet had lent Jessie were too small. She had tried everything to stretch them, but blisters had swelled on her heels. They throbbed as she tried to run.

Gray Owl noticed she was limping and aimed the lantern beam toward her feet. "Where are your moccasins?"

"I put them away for safekeeping," Jessie replied, hoping her grandfather would drop the subject.

But he persisted. "Those shoes must be hurting your feet."

"Just a little," Jessie said, biting her lip.

"Then you should go back and get your moccasins."

Jessie shook her head firmly. "No one out here wears moccasins. I want to fit in."

"Fitting in is one thing," Gray Owl remarked. "But to do it by wearing shoes that make you limp does not seem wise."

Luckily for Jessie, they had reached the barn, and her grandfather could focus on the birth of the foal instead of her tight shoes.

They hurried down the row of stalls in the barn until they reached Morning Star's. It was ablaze with light. Colonel Macintire stood between Tom and Rusty, who were both holding lanterns. Red Wolf was on his knees in the straw.

Jessie gently stroked Morning Star. "There, there, little mother," she murmured in a soothing voice. "Try to relax." Gray Owl squatted in the corner and began chanting in a low voice.

"What's he singing?" Colonel Macintire whispered to Red Wolf.

"It's a *Nimipu* song about the spring and new life," Red Wolf replied. "Very old, very good medicine."

The song had always been one of Jessie's favorites. She closed her eyes and joined in the singing. She could feel Morning Star relax.

Jessie and her grandfather continued to sing the haunting song as Red Wolf reported the progress of the birth to the ranchhands and Colonel Macintire. "I can see the foal's head and forelegs," he declared, rubbing Morning Star's side as he spoke. "You're halfway there, girl."

Jessie, still singing, opened her eyes. She could see the outline of the foal through the white birth sac. It looked as if it were asleep. Now the rest of its body was emerging.

"The foal's out!" Tom exclaimed.

Jessie stopped singing and patted the mare's neck. "Oh, Morning Star, congratulations. You've given birth to a beautiful foal."

The light from the lanterns seemed to wake the foal. It kicked out its front legs, wiggled, and twisted its head, ripping the sac wide open.

"It's out of the sac," Rusty declared. "It's a colt!"

Although the foal was wet, brown spots were already visible on his rump.

"Well, I declare," Colonel Macintire said proudly. "I believe we have ourselves a brand-new Appaloosa."

"Well done, Morning Star," Jessie murmured.

Morning Star and her new foal were still bound together by the umbilical cord as they lay in the straw. Bothered by the light, the little foal turned his head from side to side. This seemed to be a signal to Morning Star. Suddenly she began rocking her heavy body back and forth.

"She wants to stand up," Jessie said.

"Stand back and let her," Red Wolf instructed.

As Morning Star got to her feet, the umbilical cord broke. Morning Star, looking every inch the proud mother, watched over her foal as he lay in the hay, his head swaying.

"He looks so wet and cold," Jessie commented in

a voice that was filled with concern.

"Don't worry," her father said with a reassuring grin. "Morning Star will take care of that."

Morning Star gently bent her head to her newborn and warmed him with her breath. Then she methodically licked him with her dry, massaging tongue.

"He's not awake yet," Jessie giggled as the tiny foal, comforted beneath his mother's warm nostrils, sank sleepily back in the hay.

Morning Star continued to lick every part of the foal's wet hide. Red Wolf scooped up a handful of straw and helped by rubbing the foal dry.

The little foal raised his head and blinked drowsily at the world around him.

"He's so tired," Jessie cooed as the little foal's ears flopped out to the sides. "Even his ears are drooping."

As Red Wolf continued gently to massage the foal with straw, Morning Star licked the foal's nose.

"There may be some fluid from the birth in his nostrils," Red Wolf explained. "His mother is making sure he can breathe freely."

"He had better try to stand soon," Colonel Macintire murmured from his position in the corner. "They need to be on their legs within the first half hour."

The little foal cocked his head toward the ranch owner as if he'd heard him. Then he awkwardly thrust out one leg and tried to stand up. He immediately fell backwards. Then he tried both legs and failed.

Jessie giggled. "His legs are so long, they're getting all tangled."

Morning Star stood right beside the foal and gently nudged him with her nose.

"Oh, look, he's up," Tom declared, as the foal almost made it to his feet.

"Nope, he's down," Rusty corrected, as the foal collapsed back against his mother.

"He's up again!" they both cried in unison. "Nope. He's down."

After four or five more tries, with everyone cheering him on, the foal finally managed to stand. His legs were wobbly, but he steadied himself quickly.

"Good boy!" Jessie breathed a sigh of relief.

The foal turned his head, finally able to take a real look around. His eyes were bright, and even his ears were standing tall and alert. He seemed to sense his mother's closeness, which made him brave.

"Look at him," Jessie said with delight as the foal raised his head proudly. "He's a true prince."

"A very hungry prince," Red Wolf declared as the foal ducked his head under his mother's belly and

began to nurse. "Morning Star's milk will be both his food and his medicine."

"His medicine?" Jessie cocked her head toward her father. "What do you mean?"

"His mother's milk will make him strong and protect him from getting sick," Red Wolf said.

All of them watched with big grins on their faces as the tiny foal eagerly drank his mother's milk. Then he fell back in the hay, exhausted.

Colonel Macintire let loose with a full-throated laugh. "That's it, take a rest, fella. You've got a lot of work ahead of you."

Jessie looked at her father, who explained, "Colonel Macintire hopes that this foal will be the start of his new Appaloosa herd."

"The best herd since the days of Chief Joseph." The Colonel clapped Red Wolf on the shoulder. "Since you helped bring him into this world, I'd like to give you the honor of naming him."

Red Wolf lifted his chin. "Thank you, sir. It is indeed an honor."

"Give him one of your Indian names, like Flying Eagle or Leaping Fox," Colonel Macintire said with a wave of his hand. "Something with lots of spirit."

Red Wolf smiled, then turned to his daughter. "I'd like to ask for my daughter's advice. She loves horses, and she loves this mare in particular."

Jessie realized everyone in the stall was looking at her. She took a deep breath, thinking about the many names for her people. "Brave Under Fire," she murmured. "That is a name we have been given. And it certainly fits this little one's spirit."

"Or Brave Fire," Gray Owl suggested.

Jessie looked thoughtfully at the beautiful mare. Then her eyes widened and she said, "He is the son of Morning Star. I think we should use her name and call him Starfire. That is a good name for such a proud little prince."

Red Wolf looked at Colonel Macintire, who nodded. "I like it. Starfire. The Spirit of the West."

CHAPTER TEN

The Dare

"Class!" Miss Quimby tapped her long stick on the top of her heavy oak desk. "Pay attention! Jessie will now recite from *The Song of Hiawatha* by Henry Wadsworth Longfellow."

Jessie stood in front of the class, trying to keep her knees from knocking together. It was June and the children were all participating in the final exams of the year. The fourth grade's exam for the day was recitation.

Jessie wet her lips and began. "By the shores of Gitchee Gumee, by the shining Big-Sea-Water, stood the wigwam of Nokomis, daughter of the Moon, Nokomis."

Jessie suddenly went blank. She hadn't wanted to recite this poem. She'd sworn off anything that had to do with Indians while she was at school. But Miss Quimby thought the poem was appropriate.

"Jessie?" Miss Quimby asked, as Jessie swallowed several times. "Have you forgotten the poem?"

Jessie shook her head nervously. "Oh, no, Miss Quimby. It's just that my throat is a little dry."

"Get yourself a drink of water and try again," Miss Quimby instructed.

Jessie limped to the back of the room. She was still wearing the boots that Harriet had loaned her. And they still hurt.

As she scooped a drink of water from the bucket, Jessie quickly ran through the words of the poem. She knew them backward and forward. It was a bad case of nerves that was making her forget.

Once back at the head of the class, she tried to picture the images of the poem in her mind. She saw Nokomis rocking Hiawatha in his bark cradle and their little tipi nestled under giant firs on the banks of a great lake. The pictures helped her remember. This time she recited the words perfectly. And when she reached the last phrase, Miss Quimby and the entire class applauded.

"That was quite lovely, Jessie," Miss Quimby said.

"Especially the image of Ishkoodah, the comet, with his fiery tresses like a feathered headdress." She gave Jessie an encouraging smile. "And as long as we're on the subject of Indians, maybe you could tell us what it's like living in a wigwam—or tipi, as you call it."

Jessie knew that she was still being tested, but she couldn't bring herself to discuss her reservation life. As far as Jessie was concerned, she had put aside her past. There was only the present life of living on the ranch.

"I'm sorry, Miss Quimby," Jessie replied. "But I don't remember. My family lives in a regular wooden house on the Macintire ranch. I have slept out in the barn once or twice when the mares were foaling, or one of the horses had colic. I could tell you about that."

Miss Quimby adjusted her glasses. "That won't be necessary. Thank you, Jessie. You may sit down."

The children listened to Gus Shaw recite "The Raven" by Edgar Allan Poe. Then Harriet gave a spirited rendition of Rudyard Kipling's "If." Finally it was time for recess.

Jessie and Harriet joined some of the other children who were watching Floyd Perkins and Johnny Anderson play marbles under the apple tree.

As they watched, everyone chatted about the

end-of-the-year party—a picnic at Treachery Falls.

"It's on Saturday," Addie May Bruce was saying. "It's going to be so much fun!"

Harriet nodded her agreement. "Every year, Ma packs a huge picnic basket full of pies for our picnic. And after the contests we all gorge ourselves."

"Contests?" Jessie asked. "What kind of contests?"

"We have horse races and barrel racing," Harriet replied. "And last year Gus started a whole new category of trick riding."

Gus, who was keeping an eye on the game, raised his head. "I saw it at the Pendleton Roundup."

"Do you ride, Jessie?" Addie May asked.

Jessie couldn't help but brag a little. "I was the fastest rider two years in a row at the Indian Camp celebrations." She smiled, remembering how proud she had felt riding in the big parade.

Gus tossed a dirt clod at the trunk of the apple tree. "So who'd you race?"

"The other boys and girls," Jessie replied. "One at a time. By the end of the contests, your horse can get pretty tired. But Fleetfoot—that's my horse—has a strong spirit. I think he likes racing even better than I do."

"How about barrel racing?" Gus asked. "Did you ever do that?"

Jessie waved one hand casually. "Certainly. We even have a contest where you have to turn in a circle while racing bareback. The men also have to be able to shoot while hanging off the side of the horse."

"Shoot? You mean, like guns?" Harriet asked.

"No. Bows and arrows," Jessie replied. "Of course, now they don't really shoot. They just do the side-of-the-horse trick."

"This I gotta see," Gus said, shaking his head in amazement. "Will you do it for us on Saturday?"

"I wish I could," Jessie said with a frown. "But I don't have a horse."

"Where is Fleetfoot now?" Addie May asked.

"Back at the res—" Jessie caught herself. She had vowed never to mention the reservation again. "He's at my old home. We couldn't bring him to the ranch."

Floyd looked up from his marble game. "Ah, Jessie couldn't do it anyway. She's just bluffing."

"That's not true!" Jessie said, putting both hands on her hips and glaring at the heavyset boy.

Floyd shrugged. "Well, you'll never be able to prove it. You don't have a horse."

After school, Jessie stomped all the way home, with Harriet struggling to keep up with her.

"It's just so unfair," she declared, throwing her books onto an overturned pail by the pasture. "I can outride all of them."

"It isn't fair," Harriet sympathized, dropping her own books on top of Jessie's. "Maybe we should just skip the picnic, if it would make you feel better."

Jessie leaned on the fence and hung her chin miserably on the top rail. "Nothing will make me feel better except. . ." Jessie's words died in her throat. The solution to all of her problems was standing right in front of her.

"Morning Star!" she whispered. The Appaloosa mare had just trotted into the center of the pasture, with little Starfire close behind. It had been almost two months since she'd given birth to the little colt, and the mare was now sleek and trim.

"I'll ride Morning Star," Jessie said slowly. "She used to perform in front of thousands of people. Why, she could probably teach me a few tricks."

"Are you sure you want Morning Star?" Harriet asked. "You've never ridden her before."

"No, but she likes me. And there isn't a horse on this ranch that can do what Morning Star does. She's the perfect choice."

"Do you think your father will let you ride her?" Harriet whispered, wide-eyed.

"Of course. And just to get a head start, I'm going to take her for a practice ride right now."

Jessie raced to the tack room just inside the stable door where the saddles and bridles were hung. She found Morning Star's bridle on a peg just below her name.

Walking back into the pasture, Jessie whistled for Morning Star. The mare immediately stood at attention and then trotted over to meet Jessie.

"That's a good girl," Jessie murmured, slipping the bit into the horse's mouth. "What do you say we go for a ride today?"

The mare chewed at the cold bit, trying to push it out of her mouth with her tongue.

"Jessie!" her father called from the stable yard. "What do you think you're doing?"

Jessie turned, ashamed that she hadn't asked her father for permission. "I was just going to take Morning Star for a little ride in the pasture," she hurriedly explained. "I didn't think you'd mind."

Red Wolf's face was very stern. "She's not ready to be ridden yet."

"She seems fine to me," Jessie said.

"She's still nursing Starfire," her father explained. "It's better for Morning Star not to be ridden until her colt's been weaned. He's still very attached to his mother. If she goes off without him, he'll be upset."

"But it's been two months," Jessie pleaded.

"Please, Father, one little ride."

His jaw locked stubbornly. "No. You can't take her. And that's that."

All of the emotions bubbling inside her suddenly welled up. Jessie stamped her foot. "How am I going to fit in with the other children if you won't let me ride the mare?"

"Take another horse," Red Wolf countered.

"I can't. Morning Star is the only horse who knows how to do stunt riding. I have to ride Morning Star."

Red Wolf shook his head. "I don't understand."

"I'm an outsider," Jessie shouted. "I'll always be an outsider until I prove myself!" Jessie slammed the bridle onto its peg. "I wish we'd never moved to this awful place! I hate it here. Hate it!"

"Jessie! No more!" her grandfather ordered. Gray Owl stood framed in the barn door. "You must never talk to your elders like that. It's not our way."

"I don't care about *our* way," Jessie shouted, her chin quivering. "Our way is the stupid way. Our way is dead."

"Oh, Jessie, that is not true!" Red Wolf said, quietly.

"It is!" she cried, running to the door of the stable. Hot tears burned her eyes as she ran from the barn.

Behind her she heard Gray Owl calling her name.
Jessie ignored him.

Jessie stumbled blindly across the stable yard until
she reached her house. Once inside she fell on her
bed, buried her face in her pillow, and wept.

CHAPTER
ELEVEN

Giddyap, Morning Star!

The next three days were difficult ones for Jessie. Her parents had tried to talk to her about how she felt, but she hadn't wanted to discuss it. Jessie wanted only to put the whole thing behind her, resigning herself to the fact that she wouldn't be riding Morning Star, and she wouldn't be going to the picnic.

Harriet had begged her to join the school group, pointing out that not everyone had a horse to ride.

"I don't have a horse," Harriet had said. "I don't even know how to ride one. And I'm going to the picnic."

But it wasn't the same. Jessie didn't know how to explain to Harriet how much riding meant to her. "It's better if I stay home," Jessie had said finally. "Maybe I'll join the picnic next year."

Now it was Saturday and Harriet was gone.

Jessie stood in the pasture, smiling. Just being in the bright sunshine made her feel better. She held her hand out in front of her. Balanced on the center of her palm was a blue camas flower.

"Here, boy," Jessie called to Starfire, who stood with his mother at the far end of the field. "I've got a treat for you."

Starfire spotted the colorful bloom and scampered across the pasture to Jessie. He stopped a foot away and sniffed the tips of Jessie's fingers.

"Go ahead and eat it, you silly boy," she murmured to the little foal. He seemed to understand her and raised his head to look in her face. Then he very delicately picked the flower off her palm and swallowed it whole.

"You didn't even taste it!" Jessie laughed. "Now I'll have to pick you another one. And this time you had better promise to chew it."

Morning Star trotted up to Jessie's side and completely ignored her outstretched hand. The mare knew what she was looking for and playfully nipped at the pocket of Jessie's apron.

"You're right, I didn't forget you," Jessie chuckled,

putting her hand in her pocket. She pulled out a bright orange carrot for Morning Star.

"There you go, my lady," Jessie said soothingly, presenting the horse with the treat.

Morning Star ate the carrot and then threw her head back and whinnied. That sent Starfire into a flurry of motion. He raced in a broad circle around the pasture, bucking and kicking. As Rusty would have said, "jest feelin' his oats."

Jessie chuckled at the frisky colt's antics. She was feeling quite content to spend the entire Saturday with Morning Star and her foal when the foreman's son, Gus, suddenly appeared.

He had saddled his mustang pony, Lightning, and was galloping full tilt across the ranch yard. When he spotted Jessie standing by the pasture fence, he rode over and reined Lightning to a halt.

"Aren't you going to the picnic?" Gus asked.

Jessie shook her head. "No. I don't really feel like going."

Gus chuckled, then picked at his teeth with a sprig of hay. "Yeah, we all figured you wouldn't show."

"What do you mean?"

"When you did all that braggin' about what a fine rider you were, we knew you'd never go to the picnic." He grinned down at her smugly from his saddle.

"Floyd Perkins was even going to lend you his horse, just so everyone could see what a big old liar you are."

"Liar?" Jessie was horrified. She had always prided herself on telling the truth. It was humiliating to think that anyone would call her a liar.

"Why, Floyd doesn't think you can even ride a horse."

Jessie's nostrils flared angrily. "I can outride Floyd Perkins any day of the week. With my eyes closed."

"Then prove it," Gus challenged. "Come to Treachery Falls with me and show Floyd he's wrong."

"I just might do that," Jessie said through clenched teeth. "I'll show him and that whole bunch at Sunnyside School that I am not a liar."

Without hesitating, Jessie turned to Morning Star and took hold of her dark-brown mane. She swung herself onto the mare's back and nudged her sides with her heels. "Come on, Morning Star, let's show 'em."

Jessie moved the mare toward the gate, where Gus was waiting with Lightning. As she rode by the stable, Jessie leaned over and scooped up a bridle hanging on the fence rail. Once outside the pasture, she wheeled the horse around and kicked the gate shut with her foot. It swung back against the rail just as little Starfire scampered up, all ready to follow his mother.

"Be a big boy, Starfire, and stay right here," Jessie told the colt as she slipped the bridle over Morning Star's head. "Don't worry. I'll bring your mama back real soon."

The foal whinnied, then reared up on his back legs and pawed the air.

Jessie dug her heels into Morning Star's sides, and she and Gus trotted side by side out of the barnyard onto the road.

Jessie was so angry at Floyd and Gus and all the rest of them at Sunnyside School that she barely heard Starfire's shrill cries behind her. Morning Star whinnied several times and pulled her head to the side, as if she wanted to go back, but Jessie jerked the mare's head forward. "Not yet, girl. We've got work to do."

As they pounded up the hill away from the ranch, Jessie kept repeating over and over, "I'll show him. I'll show them all!"

CHAPTER
TWELVE

Picnic at Treachery Falls

Treachery Falls lived up to its name. Jessie could hear the roaring water pound over the big gray boulders for nearly a mile before she and Gus reached the falls and the picnic area.

When Jessie arrived, she was surprised to find people happy to see her. All of her schoolmates were eager to see the new girl show off her riding tricks.

Gus showed her where to tie Morning Star, who whinnied and looked restless. Then Jessie and Gus hurried to join the others.

"I didn't think you'd come," Harriet whispered as she walked with Jessie toward the broad meadow bordering the picnic area. "But I'm so glad you did!"

"Me too!" Jessie replied, waving to Fannie and Cora Carter, who were dressed in matching pink calico dresses. They were carefully arranging the picnic baskets on several red-and-white checked tablecloths that had been spread across the grass.

"I thought Red Wolf wouldn't let you ride Morning Star," Harriet said. "What happened?"

Jessie was afraid to tell Harriet everything. Instead she was vague and said, "I didn't get a chance to talk to my father. Gus suggested I ride over with him, so I did."

Harriet frowned in confusion. Finally she shrugged and looped her arm through Jessie's. "I'm so glad you made it in time. The races are just about to start."

The children on their horses were lining up for the races, which were to be flat-out sprints up and back across the broad meadow.

Jessie ran to get Morning Star. They reached the starting line just as Kevin Lucas, one of the oldest boys at Sunnyside School, was calling the first race. "On your marks. Get set. Go!"

True to her word, Jessie proved what a skilled rider she was. She and Morning Star easily won the first and second races. She placed second in the third, only because Morning Star seemed a little out of breath.

After the sprints, everyone split up into teams for the potato relay race. One-by-one the contestants had to ride as fast as they could to the end of the field, balancing a potato in a metal ladle. When they reached the other side, they had to hand the ladle to their teammate without dropping the potato.

Jessie was put on the same team as Gus Shaw and the Carter sisters. She was secretly delighted when Gus lost control of his mustang at the hand-off and dropped his potato. That made her team lose, but she didn't mind. It was all in good fun.

"Lunchtime," Harriet called after the potato races. "Come and get it!"

The picnic area lay on a sweeping curve in the river just below the torrent of the falls. A grove of cottonwoods and willows hugging the riverbank provided a welcome canopy of shade. Jessie and the others found a place on the checked tablecloths and hungrily lit into the fine lunch of fried chicken and huckleberry pie. Then it was time for the trick riding.

"All right, Jessie," Floyd Perkins jeered as he led the others back to the field where the horses were tied. "It's time to put your money where your mouth is."

Jessie was certain she could perform most of her riding tricks, but she wasn't sure if Morning Star was up to it. The mare had been sweating and out of breath during the races. Jessie hoped the break for lunch had given Morning Star enough time to rest.

"You said you could turn around in a complete circle on a horse that's galloping full steam," Gus said. "We want you to show us."

"I'll do more than that," Jessie said, trying to keep her voice sounding confident. "I just happen to have with me the star of a traveling Wild West show. I'll perform a bunch of stunts."

Jessie ran across the field to the Appaloosa mare and whispered in her ear. "Don't be nervous. Just pretend you're back again performing before your fans."

The mare raised her head and pricked her ears forward.

"That's the spirit," Jessie said, grabbing ahold of her mane and swinging onto the horse's back. "Let's show them some real riding."

All of the Sunnyside School children lined up along the edge of the meadow to watch the demonstration. Jessie waved to the crowd, then clucked her tongue and guided Morning Star in a wide circle around the open field.

She cantered around the circle first to establish a rhythm. The second time they passed the group, Jessie lay back with her head resting on the horse's rump, her hands behind her back. Then she sat up and, looping her leg over Morning Star's neck, spun around in a circle as the horse continued to canter.

Most of the children clapped their hands at this, but Floyd kept his fists shoved firmly in the pockets of his overalls.

"Here's one just for you, Floyd Perkins," Jessie whispered. She stood up on the mare's back, then shifted her feet so that she was positioned right at the rump. Keeping her arms outstretched to the sides, she rode in a circle, keeping her balance while she waved at the crowd of cheering children.

"You look like an acrobat in the circus," Harriet cried as Jessie and Morning Star cantered by.

Jessie couldn't help smiling. Morning Star was a perfect show horse. Jessie couldn't have hoped for a smoother ride.

Then Jessie dropped back down onto Morning Star's back. She guided the mare away from the circle toward a massive black oak at the edge of the meadow. The tree had a low-hanging branch that jutted straight out over the grass about six feet above the ground.

Morning Star cantered toward the tree and, as they grew nearer, Jessie stood up again.

"Doesn't she see that limb?" Fannie cried. "She's going to get knocked off her horse."

Jessie eyed the limb and bent her knees. She dared not make a mistake on this. Morning Star would be fine, but Jessie could end up with a broken leg.

Just before they reached the tree, Jessie heard Harriet scream, "Jessie, don't do it!"

Then Morning Star was close to the limb, and Jessie sprang in the air.

She heard a collective gasp from the crowd. For one exhilarating moment Jessie felt like a bird in flight. The branch passed under her, and she landed neatly on Morning Star's back.

Excited whoops and whistles split the air, as the crowd cheered. It was Floyd Perkins who cheered the loudest, waving his felt hat in the air.

Jessie's grin spread from ear to ear. She'd done the impossible. She'd won Floyd Perkins and Gus Shaw over to her side.

Suddenly the meadow was filled with her schoolmates as they ran to congratulate her. Jessie hopped off Morning Star and hugged her tightly around the neck. "You were magnificent!" she whispered.

Then the children were all around them, patting Morning Star, shaking Jessie's hand, and chattering

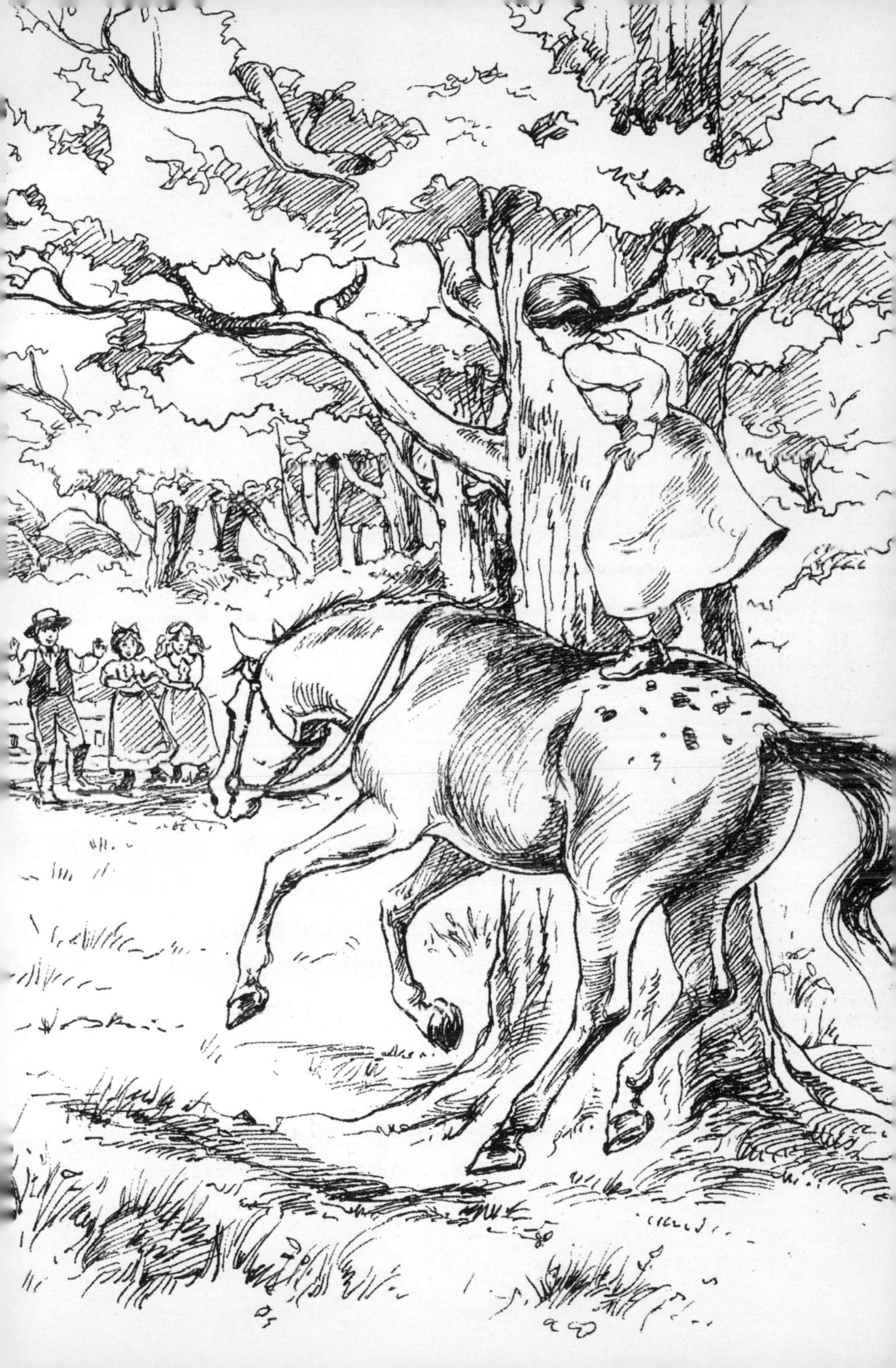

away a mile a minute.

"Say, Jessie," Floyd said, as he approached her with his hat in his hands. "Could you teach me that trick? I'd love to show my pa. Boy, would he be impressed!"

Jessie checked her horse. Morning Star was sweating and her nostrils were flaring in and out. Her sides were pumping like the bellows in a blacksmith's shop. The effort had clearly tired her. "I'd like to show you, Floyd," Jessie said, sincerely. "But Morning Star is worn out from all the riding she's had to do today. Maybe we can do it another time."

Floyd shrugged shyly. "Sure, no problem."

Then Harriet rushed forward and gave Jessie a great hug. "Oh, Jessie, you were spectacular. Everyone's raving about what a good rider you are. You should be so proud!"

Jessie did feel proud. Most of all, she felt happy to fit in with all her schoolmates.

But her joy was short-lived, as the sound of pounding hooves from a horse riding at full gallop made everyone turn their heads. Rusty was hurtling down the trail toward the picnickers.

"We've got trouble at the ranch," he cried, pulling his horse to a stop near the crowd of children. "Someone left the pasture gate open this morning, and Morning Star and Starfire are missing."

The group of children parted to reveal Jessie and Morning Star.

Rusty relaxed visibly in his saddle. "Am I relieved to find them with you, Jessie. The Colonel's 'bout to throw a fit—"

All of the color drained from Jessie's face. "I only have Morning Star," she murmured. "Starfire was back in the pasture."

Rusty frowned. "Well, he ain't there now. Didn't he go with you?"

"No. I left him behind."

"You mean it was *you* who left the gate open?"

"I thought I shut it," Jessie protested.

"Didn't you check it before you rode off?"

Jessie shook her head miserably.

"Aw, Jessie." Rusty stared at her in disbelief. "You know better than that. I don't know what the Colonel's going to do when he hears about this."

Jessie covered her face with her hands. "Oh, this is terrible. Starfire must have followed us out of the pasture. But I didn't even see him."

She really hadn't paid attention to anything. Her only thought had been on getting to the picnic and proving to the world what a great rider she was.

"Colonel Macintire's already sent Red Wolf and the

rest of the boys out to comb the hills and coulees for that colt. But that little fella could have wandered off anywhere." He looked up at the sky. "And it'll be dark soon. If he falls into one of these gullies, well. . ."

Rusty's voice trailed off. Nobody in the crowd of children said a word. They all knew what Rusty meant.

Jessie turned to Morning Star, whose ears had pricked forward. She was no longer breathing heavily. Every muscle of her body seemed to be drawn tight, as if she were a coiled spring ready to be released.

"Morning Star," Jessie murmured, looking into the horse's deep brown eyes, "It's my fault Starfire's lost. I'm so, so sorry. We have to find him. We have to."

Before Rusty could say another word, Jessie had swung onto the Appaloosa's back.

"Go, Morning Star," she urged, leaning over the mare's neck. "Go find Starfire!"

CHAPTER THIRTEEN

Lost and Afraid

Darkness covered Jessie and Morning Star like a thick blanket. They had been searching for hours but had found no sign of little Starfire.

Jessie guessed the colt had tried to follow them when they left the pasture, but quickly fell behind. She tried retracing her steps to different places along the trail where she thought the foal might have taken a wrong turn. Her first two paths had led to dead ends.

Now she was on her third attempt. As she and Morning Star followed a narrow trail along the edge of a steep cliff, her heart sank. The cliff rimmed a rushing stream that led into a thick clump of pines.

Jessie was afraid to enter the woods. The moon

was providing some light, but once they went into the woods, Jessie knew she wouldn't be able to see anything. Tears blurred her vision as she whimpered to Morning Star. "I'm so scared. What if we lose our way?"

Morning Star replied with a defiant toss of her head. Jessie leaned forward and, clinging to the mare's neck, let her lead them into the gloomy forest.

The thick brush was almost impassable. Branches and thorny vines cut at Jessie's arms and legs. She covered her face, afraid that she might be poked in the eye. "It's no good in here," Jessie moaned. "Maybe we should turn back."

But Morning Star seemed determined to push on. Slowly the sturdy horse picked her way through the dense thickets. Several times she raised her nose, sniffed the air, and whinnied. But no one responded.

Another half hour passed. Now Jessie was weeping openly, unable to control her fear and guilt. "It's all my fault," she blubbered. "I should have listened to my father. This is my punishment for trying to be someone I'm not. I should never have denied my people, or the old ways."

Jessie buried her head in Morning Star's mane and sobbed. She no longer cared if the branches slashed her face. She felt she deserved it.

Once again Morning Star raised her head, sniffed the wind, and whinnied.

This time she was answered by a pitiful cry.

"Did you hear that?" Jessie swiped at the tears clouding her vision, and strained her ears to hear.

Morning Star clattered across the stones lining a stream bed, stopping once more to whinny. This time the answer was louder.

"That way!" Jessie pointed toward a clearing just beyond an outcropping of rocks. "Oh, Morning Star, hurry."

Morning Star worked her way to the edge of the clearing, and paused.

Standing in the middle of the meadow was Starfire. He was tangled in a patch of thorny bushes. His coat was matted and wet, and even in the darkness Jessie could see that he was shivering. He spotted his mother and cried pitifully.

"Starfire!" Jessie cried. "We're coming!"

Morning Star whinnied and headed for the clearing. But the moment she reached the edge of the woods, the mare froze.

"What's wrong, girl?" Jessie said, prodding the mare with her heels. "Come on, let's go."

Morning Star's ears pressed flat against her head. She snorted nervously as she skittered in a half-circle, her eyes looking wildly about her.

"What's the matter?" Jessie whispered. "What do you hear?"

Crack.

Something was in the bushes. Jessie caught her breath and listened.

A deep growl rumbled from the brush between them and Starfire.

Jessie knew that sound well. She'd heard it several times before near the Colville Reservation.

Cougar!

She swung around to look at the little foal. He was the perfect-sized meal for a hungry mountain lion.

"No!" Jessie screamed, digging her heels into Morning Star's sides.

But the mare was frozen with fear. She stood staring at the bushes, her knees locked, not moving.

Now the cougar was out of the brush. Jessie could just make out the outline of its sleek, powerful body in the moonlight. Slowly he crept toward the colt.

"Oh, no, you don't!" Jessie bellowed, leaping off Morning Star's back. She darted right between the cougar and the foal, waving her arms in the air. She had always been taught, if she ever met a mountain lion in the woods, to make herself as big as possible and startle the cat into running away. She roared and whooped while swinging her arms and kicking out her legs.

The cougar froze and lowered his head. He was staring at her, clearly trying to determine if she was a real threat.

Jessie felt her heart pounding faster and harder than ever before. This cat was huge. He could easily take her down with a single swipe of his razor-sharp claws.

She had no weapon. The only strength she could draw upon was from inside herself. Jessie locked eyes with the cougar, and her grandfather's words echoed in her mind.

"When you look a wild animal in the eye, he will take it as a challenge," Gray Owl had said. "You must look farther, deeper. Bore a hole straight through his eye into his soul. Let him know you are chief."

Jessie took a deep breath and concentrated. She saw the cat's cold yellow eyes glinting in the moonlight and was afraid. She took another breath.

"Look deeper," a voice inside her whispered.

And she did. She looked through the yellow eyes, into the soul of the beast. And she was no longer afraid.

I am strong, she thought. *You are weak. You will*

back down. I will win.

The cougar stared at her, mesmerized. But he didn't retreat. He just stood frozen, like Morning Star. It was as if Jessie were surrounded by statues.

The pressure was unbearable. Jessie was certain her will would crack soon, and the cougar would win. She knew they were in a deadlock, but she refused to give in. They held their positions for what seemed like hours, neither one budging an inch.

As she stared, the big cat crouched low, coiled to spring.

But before he could even make a move, something huge and white dashed out of the woods.

It was a horse. But not just any horse. It was the magnificent spotted white stallion from her dream.

With an ear-splitting cry the white Appaloosa reared up on his hind legs and beat at the cougar with his forelegs. His hooves were a blur of motion, and suddenly the big cat rolled onto its back, howling in pain.

He snarled at the horse and swiped at the lightning quick hooves, but to no avail.

Over and over, the stallion beat off the mountain lion, until finally it limped away into the woods.

Morning Star raced to her foal's side, sniffing him all over to make sure he was unharmed.

The stallion turned to look at Jessie, who collapsed gratefully to her knees and closed her eyes.

"Thank you, Grandfather, for your wisdom," she murmured. "And thank you, my *wayakin*, for your help and guidance."

When she opened her eyes, the great spirit horse was gone.

Home at Last

An hour later, the very weary threesome arrived back at the ranch. All of the windows in the houses and barns were ablaze with light. It was clear that no one on the Macintire ranch was planning to sleep until Morning Star and her colt were found.

After Jessie had freed Starfire from the bushes, they had started the journey home. Jessie had walked the entire way, pausing every few miles to let Starfire and Morning Star rest. They all were cold and exhausted.

As she led the horses through the front gate, her father stepped out of the stables, a lantern in one hand.

"Wind Dancer!" he cried, running over to her. "You're safe."

Jessie was so tired she didn't realize he had called her by her Nez Percé name. "Father, I-I'm so sorry," she stammered.

"Not now," he interrupted. "Get the horses into the stable while I tell the Colonel."

Jessie could hardly stay on her feet. But she knew her father was right. She had to take care of the mare and her foal before she could even think about herself.

Jessie walked Morning Star and Starfire into their stall and gave them each a hot bran mash. Then she carefully rubbed them down, curried and brushed them, and covered each horse snugly with a blanket.

She was rubbing Morning Star's legs with liniment, in case the mare had strained any muscles, when Colonel Macintire stormed into the stable. He was followed by Red Wolf, New Moon, and Gray Owl and the ranchhands. Jessie's mother's face was lined with worry, but she made no move to go to Jessie.

"Examine those animals thoroughly, Red Wolf," the Colonel ordered. "If either one of 'em's injured, I. . . I. . ." His jaw worked soundlessly, and he shook his hands in frustration.

Jessie had never seen the Colonel so upset and angry, and she shrank back against the side of the stall. She looked to her grandfather for comfort, but he stared back impassively.

Without a word to her, Red Wolf stepped past Jessie and knelt down to look at the mare and foal. Meanwhile, the Colonel congratulated Jessie on finding his treasured colt.

"I tell you, when I find the idiot who left that gate open," he declared in his big booming voice, "there won't be a ranch west of the Rockies that'll hire that fool, that's for sure."

Jessie shot a glance at Rusty the ranchhand, who was studying one of the rafters with the greatest concentration. He had clearly not told anyone about the picnic or anything else. Jessie knew he was giving her a chance to wiggle out of her jam.

She stared down at the hay, trying to gather her courage to speak. When Jessie finally found her voice, it was scarcely above a whisper.

"I'm sorry, Colonel Macintire, I can't hide it. I'm the one who left the gate open."

"What?" the Colonel bellowed.

Jessie winced, squeezing her eyes shut. "My father told me I couldn't ride Morning Star, but I disobeyed him and did it anyway. I took her to the school picnic and must not have closed the gate tightly enough. Starfire must have followed us and gotten lost." She forced herself to look at her father's disappointed face. "If I could take it all back, I would. But I can't. And now I'm so sorry."

The Colonel's face turned redder and redder, until he looked as though he were about to explode. Then Red Wolf stood up and faced the Colonel.

"Jessie is my daughter and I am responsible for her actions," he said quietly. "If you feel you must punish her—fire me. I will understand."

The Colonel glared at Red Wolf, twirling his mustache in thought. Finally he asked, "The mare and colt—are they hurt?"

Red Wolf shook his head. "Both are in good shape. All they need is rest."

The Colonel looked around at the group gathered in the barn. No one dared to breathe. Finally he puffed out his cheeks in a big sigh. "A good night's sleep is what we all need," he declared.

Then Colonel Macintire shook Red Wolf's hand and added, "Your response to this situation is admirable. I'm glad to have you on my team."

A wave of relief washed over Jessie. At least the Colonel hadn't fired her father.

When everyone had left the stable except her father, mother, and grandfather, Jessie turned to them, waiting to be reprimanded.

It was Gray Owl who spoke first. "You have learned much tonight, Wind Dancer."

Jessie nodded sadly. "Yes, Grandfather."

"And in our tribe, when a child grows in wisdom, it is a time to celebrate."

Jessie looked up in surprise. Gray Owl's weathered face was creased in a broad smile. "You are a credit to our people."

Red Wolf nodded and embraced his daughter. "You made a serious mistake today, but it took courage to face Colonel Macintire like that and tell the truth. I am proud to have you for a daughter."

"And so am I." New Moon held out her arms and Jessie hugged her with joy. As she stood there in the stall, surrounded by the people and horses she loved most, Jessie supposed it might be possible to feel happier. But she didn't know how.

Pride of the Nez Percé

On Monday morning, Jessie arrived late to Sunnyside School. She knew that Miss Quimby wasn't fond of latecomers, but she had been helping her father with the horses. He had been so impressed by the care she'd taken with Morning Star and her foal that he'd offered to give her a few more duties on the ranch. And that morning she had prepared a poultice for a horse who had cut his foreleg.

After a brief apology to Miss Quimby, Jessie marched proudly to her seat.

"Why, Jessie!" Miss Quimby called from her place at the blackboard. "You're not limping."

Jessie nodded and smiled. "Those high-buttoned

shoes are fine for other girls," she declared. "But I'm a Nez Percé Indian. We wear moccasins on our feet."

She gestured to the beautiful beaded moccasins that had been her parting gift from her tribe. Then she held up the cornhusk bag that had been tucked away in the trunk along with the moccasins. "And we carry our important belongings in a cornhusk bag."

"What's in yours?" Harriet asked from her seat near the front of the room.

"My people believe that each one of us has a spirit guide, a *wayakin*. When we are weak, the spirit guide will bring us strength. When we are afraid, our *wayakin* gives us courage. So in my bag I keep a token of my guide." She dug in her bag and pulled out her token—a swatch of dark brown hair clipped from Morning Star's mane. "This is to remind me of my spirit guide and the true spirit of the West—the beautiful Appaloosa!"

FACTS
ABOUT THE BREED

You probably know a lot about Appaloosas from reading this book. Here are some more interesting facts about this colorful American breed.

Ω Appaloosas generally stand between 14.2 and 15.2 hands. Instead of using feet and inches, all horses are measured in hands. A hand is equal to four inches.

Ω Appaloosas come in five recognized coat patterns. A horse with a blanket pattern is dark colored in front and has a white rump or blanket. The blanket often has dark spots on it. A leopard-patterned horse is white all over and has dark, egg-shaped spots. A horse with a frost pattern has white specs on a dark background. In the marble pattern, the horse's dark coat is mixed with white hairs all over the body, but the legs and neck are a solid color. A snowflake-patterned horse has white spots all over with most of the white falling on the hips.

∩ The mane and tail of the Appaloosa are thin and do not grow very long. Their sparse hair is thought to be an asset. Their tails do not get tangled in the thorny brush that grows in their native West.

∩ An Appaloosa's spots are not just confined to the horse's coat. If you look carefully, you will see spots on the muzzle and on the skin, too.

∩ In the eighteenth century, the Nez Percé developed their breed of spotted horse from the horses that the Spanish conquistadors had brought to America about two centuries earlier.

Ω The history of spotted horses probably goes back to the very beginning of the species. Cave drawings in Europe that date back 30,000 years show horses with spotted coat patterns. And there are breeds of spotted horses in Europe today. The Knabstruper, which comes from Denmark, looks a lot like the American Appaloosa and also traces its ancestry back to Spanish horses.

Ω Appaloosas were first bred by the Nez Percé tribe in present-day Oregon and Washington State. They get their name from the Palouse River. At first a horse of this breed was called "a Palouse horse." Soon the name became "a Palousey," then "Appaloosey."

Ω When the Nez Percé were forced to move to reservations, the Appaloosa breed was almost wiped out. In 1938, the breed was revived, and the Appaloosa

Horse Club was founded in Moscow,
Idaho.

Ω The Appaloosa horse registry is the
third largest in the world. There are more
than half a million Appaloosa horses on
record, and about ten thousand new
horses are registered every year!

Ω Appaloosas are not known just for
their spots. The breed is characterized by
strong hooves, good legs, endurance, and
a sweet temperament.

Ω The Appaloosa Horse Club sponsors
four week-long trail rides for Appaloosas
and their riders, as well as an annual
National Appaloosa Horse Show and a
World Champion Show.

Ω Some people consider the Appaloosa
to be the ultimate Western horse. The
breed does excel at roping, reining, and
barrel racing, but Appaloosas can also be

found in jumper classes, in the dressage ring, on the race track, and on the polo field.

Ω There is even a whole network of horse races just for Appaloosas. These races are usually of middle distance, from 220 yards to 700 yards. Most Appaloosa races cover 350 yards of track.

Ω Appaloosas have a proud heritage based on their Nez Percé origins. Their stamina and versatility have made them one of the most popular breed of horses in the world!